Little Chimp
Is Brave

Story by Jenny Giles

Illustrations by Rachel Tonkin

A Harcourt Achieve Imprint

www.Rigby.com
1-800-531-5015

Mother Chimp went up
the big tree.

Up, up, up
went Mother Chimp.

Little Chimp ran

to the tree.

"I can go

up the big tree, too,"

he said.

Up, up, up
went Little Chimp.

"Look at me!"

said Little Chimp.

"I am up

in the big tree."

Mother Chimp went
down the tree.

"Oo! Oo! Oo!"
said Little Chimp.
"I cannot go down
the tree!"

Little Chimp looked

at Mother Chimp.

"I **can** go down

the tree!"

said Little Chimp.

"I am brave."

Little Chimp went
down, down, down
the tree.